And Then It Happened
..5..

AND THEN IT HAPPENED

·· 5 ··

M & L Wade

Books for Boys

ISBN 0-9731178-4-2

Printed in Canada

Books For Boys
P.O. Box 87
Strathroy ON N7G 3J1

This book is dedicated to all the students I've met in the past three years, and especially the following:

Aaron Adam Adrian Aidan Alex Alicia Amanda Anna Anne Anthony Antonio Ashley Austin Autumn Benjamin Bill Blake Bradley Brandon Brayden Breanne Brendon Brian Brittany Brooke Caleb Cameron Carlos Carson Carsyn Cassidy Catherine Celia Celine Charles Charlotte Chelsea Chloe Chris Christian Christina Christine Cody Cole Colin Colton Connor Craig Dakota Dalton Damien Daniel Danielle David Dawn Daria Debra Denise Derek Devin Diane Dominic Doug Dylan Edward Elicia Elija Elizabeth Emily Emma Enrique Eric Erica Ethan Evan Frank Gabriel Garrett Gary Gavin George Gordon Grant Gregory Hailey Hayden Heather Henri Holly Hunter Ian Isaac Jack Jackson Jaclyn Jake James Janessa Jared Jason Jeffrey Jenna Jennifer Jeremy Jerome Jesse Jessica John Jonathan Jordan Jose Joseph Joshua Juan Julia Julian Justin Kaitlyn Kayla Keegan Keith Ken Kevin Kiah Kian Kirsten Kristen Kyle Kylie Lauren Liam Lindsey Logan Lorenzo Lucas Luke Mackenzie Madison Maggie Manuel Marcel Marcus Mariah Marianna Mark Marlee Marnie Mason Matthew Max Megan Melissa Michael Michelle Mitchell Morgan Nathan Nicholas Nicole Noah Oliver Olivia Owen Paige Paul Payton Peter Petra Quentin Rachel Randy Reba Rebecca Renee Ricardo Richard Robert Ryan Sabrina Sam Sarah Scott Sean Selena Serena Seth Shawn Simon Spencer Stephan Steven Tanner Taylor Thomas Tiffany Tim Tina Todd Travis Trevor Tucker Turner Tyler Victor Victoria Vincent Walter Wendy Wesley William Wyatt Zachary Zoe

Contents

Chapter 1

The Supply Teacher

Our teacher, Mrs. Hoagsbrith, rarely misses a day of work due to illness. This isn't because she doesn't get sick; it's because our principal can't find a supply teacher who's willing to teach our class. Substitute teachers always ask, "Isn't that the class with Gordon in it? No, thanks. I'm busy that day." *Click.* Apparently, no amount of money can lure a supply teacher into our classroom. That's why, on Monday morning, we were all very surprised to see the principal walk into the room with a mean, older-looking man. He introduced him as Mr. Brooks, a retired teacher from the city. Mr. Brooks was very experienced and he had assured our principal that he could handle *anything*. Naturally, Gordon took that as a personal challenge.

When the principal left the room, smiling at the thought of our class having finally met its match, Mr. Brooks explained that he would be teaching us for at least a week. Mrs. Hoagsbrith was sick with a bad case of the flu, in addition to just needing a good long rest. The supply teacher looked us over with disdain. His expression suggested that he had just smelled something really bad.

Mr. Brooks cleared his throat and began. "I want you all to know that I taught for over 30 years in a large school in a big city. If I can handle city kids, I certainly can handle a bunch of small town punks like yourselves. Now, get out your math books, and let's get to work!"

I threw a glance at Gordon, who was already grinning. I knew he had a plan.

Much to my surprise and disappointment, Gordon did nothing unusual all morning. He actually behaved quite well. He was a model student. Mr. Brooks yelled at us if we so much as coughed, and he sneered at us, daring us to misbehave. No one did. All in all, it was a very dull

2

morning. At recess, we gathered around Gordon.

"Hey, why are you being so good?" demanded one kid.

"Yeah," said another. "This is the meanest supply teacher we've ever had, and you haven't done a single thing to bug him!"

"Well," said Gordon mysteriously. "I have a plan. I don't want Brooks to suspect anything, so I was just trying to throw him off by being good. When the bell rings, hurry into class as fast as you can. Things are going to get interesting!"

At the sound of the bell, our class stampeded up the stairs to the second floor. Mr. Brooks was nowhere to be seen. As everyone took their seats, Gordon hurried over to a window and opened it. Next, he took off his shoes and handed them to Paulo. He whispered some instructions to Paulo and then dashed out of the room.

Paulo stood nervously, holding Gordon's shoes upside-down out the window. The rest of us sat in our seats, squirming with anticipation.

And then it happened. Mr. Brooks entered the

classroom. He took one look at Paulo and roared, "*You! What do you think you're doing?? Get away from that window!!*" Frightened, Paulo turned around to face the angry supply teacher. He was still holding Gordon's shoes upside-down in his hands. Mr. Brooks stared at the shoes in Paulo's hands and a look of panic swept over his face. He raced to the window and looked down. Our whole class jumped out of their seats and rushed to see what had caused the supply teacher's face to turn white. Lying in a twisted heap on the ground two stories below was Gordon. His eyes were shut and he didn't move.

Speechless for the first time all morning, Mr. Brooks turned and looked at Paulo, who was still holding Gordon's shoes. His mouth hung open for a minute and then he tore out of the room yelling at the top of his lungs.

"EMERGENCY! CALL 911! GET AN AMBULANCE! SOMEBODY DROPPED A KID OUT OF THE WINDOW!!"

Teachers rushed out of their classrooms to see what the commotion was all about. Outside, we could see Mr. Brooks, Mr. Evans and several teachers rushing over to

4

the spot where Gordon had been laying. He was nowhere in sight!

Suddenly, Gordon rushed into the classroom in his socked feet.

"Quick!" he hissed. "Gimme my shoes and everybody sit down like nothing happened!" As Gordon laced up his shoes, I stole a glance out of the open window.

"He couldn't have gone far!" I heard Mr. Brooks babble. "His leg was broken, or maybe even his *neck*! I only left them alone for thirty seconds...a minute at the most. I'm gonna get sued. There goes my pension! *This is a nightmare! I'm outta here!!*" And with that, the tough city supply teacher ran to the parking lot, jumped into his car and took off in a cloud of dust, never to be seen again.

Mr. Evans turned to one of the teachers, shook his head and said, "Wow! I never saw a class drive a supply teacher crazy so fast. That's a new record, even for Gordon!"

Chapter 2

The Costume Party

It was Halloween, and in order to raise money for charity, our school was having a costume party. Not only was everyone in our school invited, but many important people, like the mayor, the Chief of Police, and the School Board Trustees had all been invited as well. The local TV network was even going to film the party for the eleven o'clock news. Everyone at Danglemore Public School was very excited, including the teachers, but no one was more excited than Gordon, Paulo and I. Our last couple of Halloweens had been very disappointing, and we were hoping that this party, complete with games, prizes and candy, would make up for all that.

Paulo's mother always made him the best Halloween costumes, and Paulo was used to winning prizes for them. This year, Mrs. Lima generously offered to make Gordon and me costumes, as well. For days we agonized over what we should dress up as, and in the end, we decided that we would all like to go as gorillas. We had seen some really cool costumes in a magazine, and Paulo's mother said they wouldn't be too difficult to make. So it was all settled. Mrs. Lima worked for two weeks on three matching gorilla costumes, complete with face masks and bunches of bananas to hang around our necks. When she was finished, we tried them on. We were unrecognizable in our three matching costumes. No one would know who we were. In fact, I couldn't even tell which gorilla was Gordon and which was Paulo.

"These are awesome!" I exclaimed. "We're gonna win a prize for sure!"

"Yeah. Thanks, Mrs. Lima. You're the best!" echoed Gordon.

We ran around the house making gorilla noises and beating our chests. Then we raced outside where we continued to make loud gorilla noises. The poor cows, who had never seen or heard anything like a gorilla before, got scared and stampeded. Kicking and mooing, they tore for the safety of the barn. Unexpectedly, they cornered Mr. Lima, who had been cleaning out the stalls, against a large pile of manure! Struggling to get away from the frightened herd, Mr. Lima slipped and fell backwards right into the pile of manure! He instantly broke into a fine chorus of swear words and threats of what he would do if he caught the three of us. Even from behind the safety of our masks, Gordon, Paulo and I didn't so much as crack a smile. He yelled at us and told us to go back into the house. We had to take off our costumes and we weren't allowed to wear them again until the costume party. Maybe someday he would look back on the situation and laugh, but I doubt it.

With still a week to go before the big party, Gordon, Paulo and I had to find some other way to amuse ourselves. We decided to concentrate on the egg launcher that we had started building in the summer. It was really just a giant sling-shot made out of ten bike innertubes tied between two trees, but we thought it would be fun to launch eggs and see how far they would go.

Paulo managed to smuggle some eggs out of the barn at his farm, and Gordon and I each took a few from our refrigerators at home. We met in the woods behind Paulo's farm and put the finishing touches on our egg launcher. It was facing the highway, and we figured that if we all pulled back on the sling-shot together, the egg might travel as far as the nearest lane.

We took an egg, carefully set it in the pouch of the sling-shot, pulled it back, and on the count of three we let it go. The egg sailed over the small bushes and shrubs and continued its flight right over the highway. It landed with a satisfying *SMACK!* on the other side of the road.

"Wow! Did you see how far that thing went?" cried Paulo. "Let's do it again!"

We launched several more eggs, and each one made it all the way across the highway. We had to wait once or twice for cars to pass, and that gave Gordon an idea.

"Wouldn't it be cool to wait for a car, and then launch an egg at just the right moment so that it sails over the car and lands on the other side of the road?"

"I don't know," I said reluctantly. "What if the egg doesn't go that far and hits the car?"

"All the eggs have gone that far," reasoned Gordon. "I say let's try it."

"I'm game," agreed Paulo, and so it was settled.

We waited for nearly ten minutes before we heard a car heading towards us. We got the egg launcher ready, and just as the car came into sight, we launched the egg. It sailed up and over the car as it whizzed past.

"Cool!" cried Paulo. "We've got to do that again!" I had to admit it was pretty fun.

"I've got a better idea!" said Gordon. "Let's wait for the next car and launch all the rest of our eggs at once!"

We counted ten remaining eggs. Carefully we loaded the pouch with all ten eggs and waited. Within five minutes we were rewarded. From the distance came the sound of a car. As it got closer, we pulled back on the sling-shot with all our might.

"Get ready!" ordered Gordon. *"NOW!"* We let go of the sling-shot, and the ten eggs flew out of the pouch.

And then it happened. The first problem was that it takes considerably more force to fling ten eggs than it does one egg, meaning that the eggs didn't go as far together as the ones we had launched singly. They smashed into the driver's side of the car. The second problem was, in our excitement, we hadn't noticed that this was no ordinary car. It was a police car, meaning that we were in big trouble!

The car squealed to a stop. Gordon, Paulo and I started to run, but a voice boomed out from the car's speaker, **"YOU THREE! STOP RIGHT THERE!"**

Slowly we turned around to face an irate police officer.

"Not *you* kids, again," he said in exasperation. "I should have known."

We were driven back to Paulo's house, where the officer personally delivered us to the front door. We were forced to tell Paulo's parents what we had been up to. Needless to say, they weren't too pleased. In fact, they were absolutely furious. Paulo was grounded for two weeks, and that included the upcoming costume party.

My parents were equally angry. When they heard that Paulo had been grounded for two weeks and was not allowed to attend the Halloween party, they thought that was a good idea. I, too, would miss the party of the year.

Oddly enough, Gordon's parents didn't seem too upset. I guess they were used to Gordon doing bad things. This wasn't by far the worst thing their son had ever done, and he got off easy. All Gordon had to do was wash the eggs off the police car and polish it until the officer was satisfied. That was his only punishment. I couldn't believe it! It wasn't fair. After all, the whole thing had been Gordon's stupid idea in the first place.

*　*　*　*　*

The rest of the week dragged by. I soon got sick of hearing kids talk about the upcoming party: what they were going to wear, what food their mothers were making, what prizes they were going to win. By Friday afternoon, I was just glad to get away from school and all the talk about the party. After dinner, I sat in my room, bored and wondering what all the other kids were doing.

I'll bet they're getting into their costumes right now, I thought. *The gym will be all decorated, and pretty soon the party will start. I hope Gordon has a lousy time. I hope he chokes on something!*

I was pulled out of my daydream by the sound of the phone ringing. My parents were out for the evening, so I reached over and grabbed it.

"Hey," said Paulo. "What are you doing?"

"Nothing," I said. "What are you doing?"

"Nothing."

There was a moment of silence.

"You know what really makes me mad?" asked Paulo, breaking the silence. "It's that Gordon is right now, at this very moment, getting ready to go to that party! The whole egg launcher idea was his, and we're the ones who got in trouble."

"I know," I agreed. "He better not win a prize for the best costume, either!"

"I'd give anything to be at that party," sighed Paulo. That gave me an idea. I must have been hanging around with Gordon too much, because I can't believe what came

13

out of my mouth.

"Hey, Paulo, are your parents at home tonight?"

"No. They're next door, having a good time, while I sit here alone."

"Mine are at a party down the street. It looks like everyone has something to do tonight but us."

"Uh-huh," agreed Paulo.

"You know, I'll bet if we just snuck out for a little while, our parents would never know the difference. We could go to the party and be back long before they come home."

"Hmmm," said Paulo. I gave him a minute to think it over. "My costume's just hanging here in my closet. It would be a shame to let it go to waste. My mom worked really hard on it."

"Great!" I shouted. "Get on your bike and meet me at my house in ten minutes!" I slammed down the receiver and grabbed my gorilla costume.

I was just coming down the stairs when the doorbell rang. I opened it, and there stood Paulo in his costume. I slammed the door behind us and we took off for the party.

14

When we arrived at the gym, it was packed with people. The music was blaring and everyone was having a good time.

"Let's find Gordon," I said, scanning the crowd for another gorilla. There were witches, ghosts, skeletons, fairies, dinosaurs, cheerleaders, monsters, and a bunch of things I couldn't identify. There was even someone dressed as a washing machine, but no gorilla.

"There he is," cried Paulo at last. *"And look at him!* Isn't that our principal he's talking to? They're *laughing!* I wonder what's so funny?"

"I think that's the Chief of Police with them. And isn't that the mayor?" I said, getting a little angry. Imagine Gordon talking and laughing with all of our enemies while he thought we were at home, grounded!

"I'll show him!" I growled. I made my way up to the little group of people that Gordon was talking to. With all the noise in the gym, I couldn't hear what they were talking about, but it sure looked like Gordon was having a good time. I swear I could see him smiling, even through his gorilla mask. I darted up behind Gordon, grabbed a

15

hold of his gorilla pants, and gave a firm yank! Then I turned and raced out of the gym as the pants dropped down around his ankles. Behind me, I could hear people laughing and shrieking as they discovered Gordon standing there in his underwear. *Serves him right,* I thought.

Outside of the gym, Paulo caught up with me.

"That'll show him!" he said. "Nice work!"

We headed home feeling very satisfied with ourselves. Neither Paulo's parents nor mine were at home when we snuck back into our own houses. No one would ever know what we had done. We couldn't wait until Monday to find out how Gordon had enjoyed the evening!

* * * * *

On Monday, the whole schoolyard was buzzing with news of the party. Everyone had had a great time, the food was fantastic, and the prizes were awesome. A lot of money was raised for charity, but the best part of the whole evening was what had happened to poor Mrs. Hoagsbrith.

"What happened to Mrs. H.?" I asked Gordon.

"I don't know," he said. "The party was too boring without you guys, so I offered Mrs. H. my gorilla costume and left early. She didn't have a costume and she said she really liked mine, so I told her she could borrow it for the night. It fit her perfectly and she seemed really happy."

Uh-oh! I thought. Aloud I asked, "So you weren't at the party at say, around nine o'clock?"

"No. I was home watching TV by then."

"You didn't talk to the principal and the mayor and the Chief of Police before you left?" I asked, beginning to sweat a little.

"No. Why would I wanna talk to *them*?" he asked, bewildered.

"No reason. Just asking!" I stammered. I shot Paulo a glance that said, *Don't say a word,* but it was too late. Paulo was on the ground laughing.

"You...pulled down...the teacher's pants!" he managed to gasp between fits of laughter.

I felt *awful.* I turned red with embarassment.

17

"Nice going," laughed Gordon when we explained what had happened. "That sure beats anything I've ever done to her!"

It was a Halloween we would never forget, and neither would Mrs. Hoagsbrith and half the town!

Chapter 3

The Three Little Pigs

"Do you ever wonder what teachers actually do on PD days?" asked Gordon one day.

"Not really," replied Paulo.

"Yeah. As long as we get a day off, who cares what they do," I said.

"Well, I've been thinking about it. I'll bet they have secret ceremonies where they make voodoo dolls of their students and stick pins in us and cast spells on us," said Gordon. Paulo and I laughed. The idea of Mrs. Hoagsbrith and the other teachers crouched over voodoo dolls with pins in their hands was pretty funny.

"That's crazy," said Paulo. "I mean, what did we ever do to them?"

Hmmm, I thought. *Well, just last week I had mistaken my teacher for Gordon and pulled down the pants of her gorilla costume in public.* The three of us became silent as we thought of the many, many reasons why our teachers might want to use black magic against us. We finally came to the conclusion that even if our teachers *did* want to use black magic against us, they probably weren't allowed to. Personally, I felt a little better.

That brought us back to wondering what teachers actually did on PD days. Without a classroom full of students, they were probably bored and just wandered aimlessly around the halls in their pyjamas. They would drink coffee and dream of Monday when their classrooms would be filled with students again.

"Hey, I've got a great idea!" Gordon suddenly cried out. He explained his plan to Paulo and me, and we laughed so hard we could barely breathe. Paulo started to choke and he sprayed orange pop out of his nose, which made us laugh even harder.

The days crawled by as we organized our plan and waited for the next PD day. At last it arrived. We met at

Paulo's house right after his parents left for work and headed to the barn. We selected 3 small piglets and with a washable marker, we drew a large #1 on the first one, #2 on the second one, and #4 on the third one. Then we put the pigs into a large crate, loaded it onto a wagon that was attached to Paulo's bike, and the three of us rode to school.

We stopped at the far end of the school yard and hid behind a large hill. From there we watched as the teachers arrived. They all went in the same door by the gym, so we figured that the other doors must be locked. As soon as we were sure that all the teachers had arrived and were safely inside the building, we quickly pulled the wagon up to the gym doors. I held the door open as Gordon and Paulo quickly unlatched the crate and herded the three little pigs into the building. Then we ran for cover in the bushes beside a large window where we could watch what was happening in the school.

At first all was quiet, and then it happened. The pigs, who were used to being in a pen all day, started to explore the school. They ran in all directions, in and out of

21

classrooms, squealing loudly. Outside the building, Gordon, Paulo and I could hear them. Suddenly, the door to the teachers' room burst open, and out came the startled teachers and our principal, Mr. Evans. They, too, had heard the noise and came out to investigate. The sight of pigs running around the school sniffing and snorting certainly got a great response from the teachers who thought they had seen it all. They started yelling and shouting, which only scared the pigs and made them run faster. One little pig darted into the library and was quickly followed by the librarian and several teachers. They cornered the pig in the computer lab and our gym teacher tackled the little porker.

"Hey! There's a #2 written on its back," he said, struggling to hold the pig down. The principal came in then with a skipping rope which he looped around the pig's neck. Number Two was led squealing down the hall and locked in the principal's office.

Half an hour later, Pig #4 was caught in the girls' change room. He, too, was taken to the principal's office.

"Well," said Mr. Evans, wiping sweat from his bald

22

head and breathing hard. "That still leaves two more pigs on the loose."

An hour later, we saw them lead #1 into the office and lock him in with the others. Before he left, Mr. Evans opened the window to air out the small room, which was becoming quite ripe with the smell of the piglets. Then he joined the teachers in the search for Pig #3.

While the teachers ran around the school frantically looking for the nonexistent Pig #3, Gordon, Paulo and I quietly parked our bikes outside the principal's office. Paulo climbed through the open window and gently lifted the pigs out, one by one, and handed them to Gordon and me.

"Hurry up!" I urged.

"Yeah. We don't want to get caught," said Gordon. Our teachers were probably hot and sweaty from chasing pigs all morning, and I guessed that they probably weren't in the best mood by now.

When the last piglet was safely locked in the crate, we jumped on our bikes and took off for Paulo's farm. We returned the little pigs back to their pen and washed off the numbers. Then we fed them a well-deserved meal and spent the rest of our day happily playing computer games while the teachers continued to hunt for the third little pig.

Chapter 4

The Giant Cupcakes

My mom is known around town as a very good cook. She is especially famous for her Giant Cupcakes, so whenever our school has a bake sale to raise money, everyone looks forward to my mom's specialty. Her Giant Cupcakes are always the first thing to sell out. This year, the PTA was hosting a bake sale after school hours, starting at five o'clock in the afternoon. My mom had agreed to make three Giant Cupcakes, and Gordon, Paulo and I sat in the kitchen watching her ice them and top each one with a cherry.

"There!" she said with a satisfied sigh when she had finished. "Now, I have to drive your sister to hockey practice, so you boys will have to walk these over to the school gym for me." She placed the Giant Cupcakes carefully on a tray.

"No problem," I said. "Can we eat the extra icing?"

"Alright," she said as she left with my sister. I grabbed three spoons from the kitchen drawer and Gordon, Paulo and I were just about to dig into the bowl of chocolate icing when Paulo said, "What's that scratching noise?"

Gordon and I looked around. The noise was coming from outside.

"It's Chopper!" exclaimed Gordon, going over to the sliding porch door and letting his dog into our kitchen. "How did you get here?" Gordon asked his dog.

"He must have followed you and waited outside for my mom to leave," I said. "Chopper's a smart dog. He knows she doesn't like him."

"What do you mean she doesn't like him?" demanded Gordon, offended. "What's not to love about Chopper?"

Before I could answer, Chopper, who had the nose of a blood hound, sniffed out the Giant Cupcakes, and in a single bound, leapt onto the table where the cupcakes stood. Both the table and the cupcakes came crashing down, and Chopper quickly pounced on the delicious treats.

"Get away from there!" I shouted. "Gordon, call off your dog! He's eating the Giant Cupcakes!"

It took the effort of both Paulo and Gordon to drag the hungry dog away from the cupcakes.

"Get him outside!" I ordered, opening the door. When Chopper was safely outside, I turned to survey the damage. There was chocolate all over the floor and the wall and the tray was empty! All that was left of the Giant Cupcakes was a few crumbs.

"Gee, I hope all that chocolate doesn't make Chopper sick," said Gordon with concern.

"Is that all you can say?" I hollered. "My mom's going to kill us! And look at this mess!!"

Suddenly Gordon snapped his fingers and shouted, "Wait! I have an idea!" He ran down the hall and into the bathroom. A minute later he returned with three rolls of toilet paper, still in their plastic wrapping, and held one up.

27

"Look," he said. "It's almost the exact same size." I didn't think I was going to like what came next.

"No, Gordon. We can't!" I said.

"No one will know the difference. There's enough icing left over to cover these three rolls. We'll bring these fake ones to the bake sale, and then we'll just have to buy them back before anyone else gets to them. Your mom will never know."

Against my better judgment, Gordon, Paulo and I each took a roll of toilet paper and began covering it with the leftover chocolate icing. When we were done, we put a cherry on top of each one and stood back to admire our work. They looked almost as good as the ones my mom had made. Maybe Gordon's crazy plan would work after all. We placed them carefully onto the tray, quickly cleaned up the mess and headed to school.

"Now," said Gordon as we entered the gym, "all we have to do is make sure we're the first ones in line and then run over and buy these fake cupcakes."

We placed our box containing the cupcakes at the end of a long table where they would be easy to find. As we

28

left the gym, we saw my mom coming in. It was her job to collect the money from the bake sale. She looked relieved to see her Giant Cupcakes sitting on a table with the other desserts.

Gordon, Paulo and I had to wait outside the gym doors along with everyone else until exactly five o'clock when the sale began. Finally the doors were thrown open and we hurried inside. And then it happened. Our principal, Mr. Evans, was standing at the gym exit handing my mom some money. In his hand was the box containing three rolls of toilet paper, carefully covered in chocolate icing and topped with a cherry! He was laughing and talking to my mom. "I've heard great things about your baking! I can't wait to try your Giant Cupcakes. I came early just to make sure I got them. My wife and I are having guests for dinner tonight, and she told me to bring something special home for dessert."

"Why, thank you!" said my mom, beaming with pride. "I hope you and your guests enjoy them. There's a secret ingredient, and I'll bet you've never tasted anything like it before!"

29

"You can say that again," whispered Gordon as the three of us stood rooted to the spot. There was nothing we could do. We watched as our principal left the gym and went home to his dinner party, where he would serve his guests chocolate covered toilet paper with a cherry on top!

Chapter 5

The Needle

On Monday morning our principal, Mr. Evans, announced that flu shots would be given to all students on Wednesday. There would be no exceptions; Even the teachers were to get needles due to the recent outbreak of a severe flu virus. When we heard the announcement, the whole class groaned. Nobody liked getting needles.

I dreaded coming to school on Wednesday, but as it turned out, I wouldn't have missed Wednesday for anything in the world. It turned out to be one of the funniest days we would ever have at Danglemore Public School.

Wednesday morning started just like any other morning, with the National Anthem and announcements, but then we found out that our teacher had volunteered our class to be the first to get their needles. She wanted to get it over with and get on with the rest of the day, she told us. Shortly after nine, our class was called down to the teachers' workroom, which had been temporarily set up as a nurse's station. No one wanted to be the first to get their needle, and nervous kids kept leaving the front of the line to take a spot at the end. Gordon, Paulo and I found ourselves getting dangerously close to the front of the line when two things happened simultaneously. The kid in front of Gordon ran to the back of the line, leaving Gordon first, and the nurse came out of the workroom to get the first kid.

"Me?" gulped Gordon. "But…"

"No buts. We haven't got all day," said Mr. Evans, coming out of his office. "You're first, Gordon. It's up to you to set an example for the others. And just to show everyone that there's nothing to it, I'll go immediately after you." He motioned Gordon into the room. With a heavy sigh, Gordon trudged in and closed the door behind him. Mr. Evans took his place at the head of our line. Once inside the room, the nurse helped Gordon roll up his sleeve. She gently pricked his arm with the needle and then placed a cotton ball over the area. After a few seconds, Gordon was told he could roll down his sleeve and tell the next person to come in. The nurse turned around to prepare the next needle. And then it happened. An idea flashed into Gordon's brain, and he quickly unzipped his jeans and undid his belt. As he walked back into the hallway where the rest of us waited, he zipped up and did up his belt.

"Nothing to it," he said as he rubbed his rear end. "I hardly felt a thing." Everyone groaned as we realized where we would get our needle. Mr. Evans, however, was determined to set a good example for the rest of us, so he calmly entered the nurse's station and closed the door. The nurse was still getting the needle ready, so Mr. Evans dropped his trousers and boxer shorts, leaned over the table and said, "OK, I'm ready." The nurse turned around, took one look at our principal with his shorts around his ankles and screamed! Teachers came running from all directions and flew into the workroom to see what the commotion was all about. Kids peered into the room, anxious to see for themselves what had caused the nurse to scream. We all watched as a red-faced Mr. Evans quickly pulled up his trousers and sputtered an apology to the flustered nurse. Then he stormed out of the workroom muttering to himself. I can't be sure, but it sounded something like, "How many more years 'til that kid graduates?"

After that, even getting a needle in the arm didn't seem so bad. To this day, I still chuckle whenever it's announced that we have to get a needle at school.

Chapter 6

The Blizzard

The blizzard started with little warning at nine o'clock in the morning, just as the school bell rang. Throughout the morning, the snow began to fall in heavy white flakes the size of jawbreakers, and the wind wasn't just howling, it was actually screaming. By ten o'clock, we couldn't see the parking lot from our classroom window. We were kept inside at recess, and by noon, the snow had drifted a metre high in the playground.

Our principal, Mr. Evans, made an announcement and told us that we were caught in the middle of an unexpected blizzard, possibly the worst snow storm in a century. We spent the entire lunch hour inside playing games and marveling at the snow as it continued to fall while our teachers wore worried expressions on their faces.

"Maybe we'll be snowed in!" one kid said excitedly, and I heard our teacher groan. While there had been many days in the past that kids and teachers couldn't get to school in the morning due to heavy snow and ice, there had never once been a time when we couldn't get *out* of school. Last year, after a day-long snowfall, we watched as our brave teacher, Mrs. Hoagsbrith, drove her car at high speed right through a snow drift that had trapped everyone, including our buses, in the parking lot. The rest of the teachers followed quickly in her path. No doubt they wanted to make sure our buses could get safely through. We were touched by our teacher's heroism and dedication to her students.

As the school day was drawing to an end, the principal made another announcement.

"The storm is getting worse. Everything in town is shutting down, and the police are closing the roads. The buses can't get through to the school, and we're afraid that the walkers will be lost in the blizzard if we send

36

them home." There was a loud sigh followed by a moment or two of silence. Then our principal continued in a shaky voice, "Danglemore Public School is snowed in."

Instantly there arose a loud, spontaneous cheer from every classroom. Mrs. Hoagsbrith opened her special drawer, took out a bottle of aspirin and swallowed two.

"Hey, Mrs. H! Why can't I go home? My house is just around the corner," said Gordon. "I'm sure I could make it. We don't have any food here. And what if the power goes out? Where will we sleep? There are no blankets and pillows!"

Our teacher looked at her aspirin bottle as if trying to decide between taking a third one and rationing them in case we were snowed in for a long time.

"You heard Mr. Evans, Gordon. No one is allowed to leave, as much as I'd like to see you all go," she replied wearily.

"Well, at least you can't give us any homework, since we're not going home. That would be illegal or something, wouldn't it?" persisted Gordon. Mrs.

Hoagsbrith swallowed a third aspirin.

A few minutes later our principal was back on the PA system asking for all teachers to come to the staff room for an emergency meeting. Then he told us that he had a special assignment for the whole school. We were to come up with an emergency plan. What would we eat? How would we stay warm? Where would we sleep? There would be prizes for the best ideas.

When Mrs. Hoagsbrith left the classroom, Gordon jumped up and grabbed a piece of chalk. He assumed the role of class leader.

"Alright, guys," he said, facing the class. "You heard the principal. We need an emergency plan."

"Aw, come on, Gordon. This is stupid," said a voice from the back of the class. "There's no food and blankets in the school. What are we gonna do? Eat each other like those people in the plane crash did?" Everyone cracked up. Before our class could begin to draw up emergency plans, our teacher came back and told us all to line up. We were going to the gym.

The whole school watched movies for the next two

hours. I had to admit that I was getting bored and hungry. Being snowed in wasn't nearly as much fun as I thought it would be. For dinner, everyone was given a chocolate bar from the grade eight class. They had been selling them to raise money for their class trip.

A few hours later, the principal announced that it was time for bed. The kids would sleep in the gym, and the teachers would sleep in the staff lounge.

"I'm still hungry," complained Gordon. "What do you say we make a break for it when everyone's asleep? We'll go to my house and get some real food."

"Sounds good to me," said Paulo, his stomach rumbling.

"Count me in," I echoed.

It took a lot longer than we thought before things quieted down in the gym. Mats had been spread out on the floor, but there weren't enough to go around. The rest of us had to sleep on our coats. We wore our hats for warmth and used our gym bags for pillows.

Finally, at about midnight, Gordon, Paulo and I made our escape. We tried three sets of doors before we found one that wasn't locked. The snow continued to fall outside and it was freezing cold, but the wind had died down a little. It was difficult to walk through the deep snowdrifts, but we didn't have far to go.

It took us nearly half an hour to trudge through the waist-high drifts, but we finally arrived at Gordon's house at around 12:30 in the morning. The house was dark; The Smith's were snowed in at work.

"How are we going to get in?" I asked.

"There's a key hidden by the back door," said Gordon.

"Good luck finding it in all this snow," said Paulo.

After about 5 minutes of searching and digging, Gordon found the key and let us into the warm, dark house.

"Thank goodness!" he whispered. "Now, let's get some real food."

We raided the fridge and the pantry and ate like starving men who hadn't seen food for five days.

"Hey!" said Paulo, reaching into the fridge and pulling out a cold bottle of beer. "I'll bet we could sell this for a small fortune right about now in the teacher's lounge."

"That's a great idea!" said Gordon. "Let's take some food back to school and sell it to the other kids! We'll get rich!"

"What if we get caught? We weren't supposed to leave in the first place!" I protested.

"We won't get caught," said Gordon firmly. "Just think about the money!"

We filled three pillowcases with food and headed back to school. Our tracks were almost completely covered over with new snow and by the time we arrived, we were soaked to the skin. My teeth were chattering and Paulo's lips were turning blue. Fortunately, the door was still unlocked and Gordon, Paulo and I tiptoed into the building. We were covered in snow, and most of it came in with us on our clothes and boots. We shook it off the best we could and snuck back into the gym with our pillowcases of food. We immediately woke up some of the kids and set up shop.

In no time at all there was a long line of hungry kids clambering to buy food. The money poured in and soon we had made $64.38. *Awesome!* With all of our food sold, we put on our coats and were about to go on a second food raid, this time to my house, and then it happened. One of the teachers in the staff lounge got up to go to the bathroom. She was not expecting the floor in the hallway to be covered with melted snow, and she slipped and fell, crying out loudly. Her surprised yell woke the other teachers, who stumbled out of the staff lounge. Mr. Evans and Mrs. Hoagsbrith took one look at the water on the floor leading from the exit to the gym, and they both muttered "*Gordon*" under their breath. They marched into the gym to investigate just as Gordon, Paulo and I were about to sneak out of the gym.

"Hold it right there, you three!" yelled Mr. Evans. "Where do you think you're going?"

Looking past the principal into the gym, Mrs. Hoagsbrith noticed food wrappers and pop cans littering the floor.

"Where did all this food come from?" she demanded.

Gordon, Paulo and I quickly explained that we had bravely weathered the storm to go out and bring food to the starving students. We tried to make ourselves sound as heroic as possible. Neither the teacher nor the principal thought we were brave.

"You could have been killed," said Mrs. Hoagsbrith. "You could have frozen to death!"

It was decided that Gordon, Paulo and I couldn't be trusted to sleep in the gym with the other students. We were taken to the teachers' lounge where we were forced to sleep on a mat sandwiched between the teachers. Gordon had to sleep with the principal on one side of him and Mrs. Hoagsbrith on the other! It was a long night.

The next morning, we awoke to sunny skies. The snow had stopped early in the morning and the plows were out in full force. Parents were able to pick their kids up from school, and Gordon, Paulo and I left the building sixty-four dollars and thirty eight cents richer. The storm of the century was over.

Chapter 7

Ice Fishing

One day during spring break, Gordon's Uncle Ivan took the three of us ice fishing. We drove out about two kilometres on the ice before we reached his hut, and then the four of us spent a great day fishing. It was so warm that we didn't even need to light the stove in the hut, and the fish were really biting. Before we knew it, it was three o'clock in the afternoon and Uncle Ivan said it was time to go home. We couldn't wait to have fresh fish for dinner!

When we stepped out of the darkened hut into the bright sunshine, we were shocked to see that the rear tires on Uncle Ivan's truck had sunk partway into the ice. We listened in awe as Uncle Ivan colourfully commented on the situation. When he calmed down and stopped cursing, he said,

"This warm weather is causing the ice to break up! Luckily I have 4-wheel drive. I'll probably be able to drive right out of that hole, but I don't want you guys in the truck with me in case we break through the ice and sink to the bottom of the lake. It's just too dangerous."

We noticed that there were some small open patches of water between us and the shore. Uncle Ivan said it would be our job to walk ahead of the truck so he could keep an eye on us and so that we could make sure that the ice was thick enough to support the weight of the truck. I wasn't too crazy about this plan, but Gordon and Paulo started walking, so I reluctantly joined them. Uncle Ivan followed at a safe distance in his truck.

We were about halfway to shore and things were going well. The three of us ran and slid along the ice, and behind us we could hear the faint sound of the radio blaring away in the truck… and then it happened. We heard a loud *CRACK!* The ice beneath our feet was breaking up! Gordon turned around and waved for the truck to stop, but his uncle mistook the gesture for a friendly wave. He waved back and continued driving toward us. Inside the truck with the radio turned up, Uncle Ivan couldn't hear the sound of the ice breaking up! Not wanting to let the truck get too close to us in case it broke through the ice and took us with it to the bottom of the lake, the three of us sped up. Uncle Ivan sped up to keep pace with us! There was another cracking sound, and Gordon, Paulo and I raced toward shore. I stole a quick glance at the truck over my shoulder, and Uncle Ivan waved at me and smiled. He thought we were just running for fun, not for our lives! We finished the last quarter kilometre in a full-out sprint, and collapsed on the shore gasping for breath, lucky to be alive!

Completely unaware of what had just happened, Uncle Ivan pulled up beside us, rolled down the window and said,

"Well, I guess I was worried about nothing. Now quit fooling around, you guys, and get in the truck. We don't want to be late for dinner!"

Chapter 8

The Joke's On Us

Last year Gordon, Paulo and I celebrated the arrival of April like we always did, with prank phone calls to the zoo. Early in the morning, Gordon phoned the zoo and asked to speak to Mr. Jim Panzee. The zoo attendant said, "I'm sorry, but we don't have a Jim Panzee working here."

"Are you sure? Check the Monkey House!" Gordon laughed as he hung up.

Moments later, Paulo called the zoo and politely asked to talk to Mr. G. Raff. This time the zoo attendant swore and hung up. Then it was my turn. I phoned and said,

"I'd like to leave a message for Mr. L. E. Font." By now, the person answering the phone was getting good and mad, but that was nothing compared to his anger after we continued to phone throughout the day asking to speak to Al Gator, Don Key, Anna Conda, Sue Keeper, and Bob Katz. By the time we were done, the man answering the phone was yelling threats and cursing at us. Satisfied that we had done our April Fool's duty, we stopped calling.

This year, however, Gordon came up with the greatest prank ever. It outdid even his wildest schemes of the past. April Fool's fell on a Saturday this year. At first we were all a little disappointed not to be in school on April Fool's Day. We could have pulled off some really spectacular stunt that would make our teachers question why they ever went into the teaching profession in the first place. After Gordon told us his amazing plan, however, we forgot our disappointment and readily agreed to help him pull it off. The joke was simple. Gordon, Paulo and I were going to trick Gordon's parents into thinking that a thief had broken into their house and robbed them.

Phase One of his plan called for a sleepover at my house on Friday night. Both Paulo's and Gordon's parents gave their permission.

Phase Two was simple; all we had to do was wait for my parents and my sister to fall asleep. The three of us were downstairs playing computer games while my family watched TV upstairs. Around eleven o'clock we heard them turn off the TV and my father and sister went upstairs to bed. My mother came downstairs to check on us, and we made a big deal of rolling out our sleeping bags, yawning and pretending to be tired. When she was satisfied that we were safely tucked in, she said good-night, turned out the lights and went up to bed. I counted to ten and then jumped up, turned on the light and tiptoed over to the furnace. Long ago I had discovered that by holding my ear to the furnace vent I could hear everything my parents said in their bedroom. Sure enough, I heard my mother say, "They were very tired. They went to bed with no arguments. They were actually pretty good tonight. Good-night, dear." Perfect. They suspected nothing.

Phase Three was a little harder. Gordon, Paulo and I had to stay awake for several hours to be extra sure that my family and Gordon's were sound asleep. At about 2 a.m., we silently tiptoed upstairs and out the kitchen door. We quietly took our bikes out of hiding beside the garage and quickly pedalled down the street to Gordon's house.

Phase Four was the trickiest by far. Leaning our bikes up against his house, Gordon pulled out his key and wordlessly let us inside. Gordon, Paulo and I silently moved throughout the house picking up objects and carrying them into the garage, where we hid them in the loft. When we were done, the DVD player, microwave oven, laptop computer and stereo had all been removed. We even took the picture off the dining room wall. The last things Gordon took were the phones. He didn't want his parents calling the police before we had a chance to yell "April Fool's!" and see the look on their faces when they realized that they *hadn't* been robbed after all.

We pedaled back to my house, let ourselves back in through the kitchen door, and tiptoed downstairs. We could just imagine the looks on Mr. and Mrs. Smith's faces when they woke up and discovered that they had been robbed during the night. It was the perfect April Fool's prank. Gordon was a genius.

Naturally, Phase Five called for us to get up early and bike over to the Smith's house in order to watch the excitement and then yell "April Fool's!" at the top of our lungs. Sounds easy, right? Wrong!! When you've spent half the night riding around the neighbourhood and robbing a house, you become exhausted. When you're exhausted, you're bound to sleep in a little longer than usual – maybe even until 10:00 or so. By then, normal people who've spent the night tucked warmly in their beds sound asleep are already up. They've noticed that they've been robbed. They've also noticed that the thief took their phones, but were relieved to discover that the thief wasn't smart enough to think about taking their cell phone, too. Thank goodness, because they are able to call the police right away. That's how come there happened to be two police cars in the driveway when we arrived at the Smith house at quarter after ten the next morning.

I skidded to a stop at the foot of the driveway. *Boy,*

Gordon is really in trouble now, I thought. Aloud I said, "Well, Gordon, good luck with the joke. Tell me how it turns out. I gotta go. I'm late for....*something!*"

"OH, NO!" he shouted, grabbing me by the shirt. "You're in on this, too. We **all** are!" he said, looking at Paulo, in case he had any plans of deserting Gordon as well.

Just then the door to the Smith house flew open and Gordon's mother came running outside.

"Oh, Gordon! Something terrible's happened!" she cried. "We were robbed last night!!"

"What? Robbed?" said Gordon, faking innocence. Years of practice had made him very convincing. Two police officers and the Chief of Police came out of the house then, followed by Mr. Smith.

The first police officer flipped open a small notebook.

"It seems that the thief or thieves entered the house through the back door. They must have cased the joint ahead of time because they knew exactly what they were after. They took a computer with a brand new game system, a portable TV, and a stereo, all from the upstairs bedroom. Nothing else seems to have been disturbed."

"Hey, that's all *my* stuff!" cried Gordon, looking suspiciously at Paulo and me. And then it happened.

"But that's impossible!" I said. "Paulo and I didn't go near your bedroom! We only took what you told us to take." Instantly I slapped my hand over my mouth. I had let the cat out of the bag!

"Shut up!" hissed Paulo, but it was too late. The police and Gordon's parents had heard every word, and they knew that we were the thieves.

"HA! APRIL FOOL'S!!" shouted Gordon's dad.

"But how did you know it was us?" asked Gordon, bewildered.

"If you think I can't hear three kids breaking into my own house, you're wrong. I watched the whole thing from our bedroom window. I figured out what you were up to, and I thought I'd pull a little prank of my own. The police agreed that it was time to teach you kids a lesson, so they came over to watch the fun this morning." Turning to the police officers, he said, "Thanks for stopping by."

"Any time, Mr. Smith," said the Chief.

When the officers left, Mr. Smith burst into laughter and said, "You boys should know better than to mess with me - the King of April Fool's. By the way, Gordon. You can have all your stuff back in two weeks! And you and your friends can carry all of *our* things back into the house and put them back where they belong!"

Chapter 9

To Catch A Thief

On Monday morning, Mrs. Hoagsbrith entered the classroom and announced that she had some bad news.

"I took a little trip over the weekend. When I got off the train, I set my bags down for a second, and when I turned around to pick them up, someone had stolen my new leather school bag!"

Gordon, who sits right next to the teacher's desk, turned around and grinned at Paulo and me. Gordon always likes it when bad things happen to good teachers.

"Turn around, Gordon. The problem is," continued Mrs. Hoagsbrith, "that I had taken your english tests along with me to mark. They were in my school bag, so

I'm afraid that means that you will all have to rewrite the test. I need those marks for report cards next week."

Gordon turned around again, but this time his grin had disappeared. Gordon always hates it when bad things happen to good students.

"Face the front, Gordon!" said the teacher sharply. "Now, I will give you a full week to study for the new test. You will have to rewrite it next Monday. That even gives you the weekend." There were sighs and groans from the class.

"I'm sorry," Mrs. Hoagsbrith apologized. "But I don't know what else can be done."

At lunch time, Gordon announced that he had a plan that might get us out of rewriting the english test.

"We'll go down to the bus station ourselves and see if anyone turned in a leather school bag full of tests. We'll check the lost and found, and maybe we can even offer a reward if anyone finds it."

"But where'll we get the money for the reward?" I asked.

"We'll worry about that later. The important thing is

to get those tests back so we don't have to waste a perfectly good weekend studying."

After school, Gordon, Paulo and I biked to the train station and asked the clerk if anyone had found a leather school bag.

"Sorry, boys. There's nothing in the Lost & Found," he said after he checked a small room behind his desk. "But your teacher isn't alone. Lots of things are stolen everyday. People aren't very careful with their bags and packages, I'm afraid."

"Lots of things are stolen everyday," repeated Gordon thoughtfully.

"Just today, two briefcases and a laptop computer were reported stolen. There's a clever thief on the loose, that's for sure."

We thanked the man, got on our bikes and headed home. As we pedalled, Gordon said, "If only we could find the thief who took our tests, we wouldn't have to waste all that time studying again."

"But how are we going to do that, Gordon?" asked Paulo. "We're not detectives."

"No, but I have a plan," said Gordon. Paulo and I glanced at each other warily. We were all too familiar with Gordon's plans.

Against our better judgment, we listened to Gordon's plan and then followed him on our bikes to the town dump. We sifted through heaps of rotting garbage, old appliances and broken furniture until we found exactly what we were looking for - a large suitcase.

Balancing the suitcase on my handlebars, we rode back to my house and carried the suitcase up to my tree fort. Carefully we cut two small holes in one side of the suitcase – one to breathe through and one to see out of. Our plan was quite simple. We would put Gordon into the suitcase and leave him in the train station on Saturday, when it was bound to be busy. Gordon would be able to watch out for anyone who looked suspicious, and maybe he would even catch the thief in action. Then we could call the police, identify the crook, and hopefully get Mrs. Hoagsbrith's school bag (and our tests) back. It might even earn us a few extra marks on our report cards.

Early Saturday morning we rode our bikes, with the

empty suitcase, over to the train station. When no one was looking, Gordon quickly climbed inside and Paulo and I zipped it up. With all the other suitcases littering the floor, ours blended right in. Paulo and I sat down on some nearby benches to help Gordon keep a lookout. Our plan was to stay for a few minutes to make sure that Gordon was OK. Then Paulo and I would come back later to unzip him and see if he had discovered who the thief was. After about fifteen minutes, we decided it was time to leave Gordon on his own. We stood up to go, and then it happened. A man jumped out of a dark coloured pickup truck. He rushed into the train station and grabbed two suitcases – a new-looking leather one, and the one containing Gordon. He quickly dragged them outside and dumped them into his truck. Then he climbed into the cab, turned the key in the ignition, and floored it out of the parking lot! Gordon had been stolen!!

For a few seconds, Paulo and I were too stunned to do anything but stare in the direction the truck had gone. Then Paulo yelled, "Come on! We've got to save Gordon!"

We raced outside and grabbed our bikes. Pedalling with all our might, we chased after the truck. It turned left and we followed it and then suddenly, the truck was gone. It had sped up and disappeared from view. Paulo and I rode up and down the street, searching parking lots, driveways and side streets, but there was no sign of the dark pickup truck.

"It's no use," I panted. "We'll have to call the police and tell them that Gordon's been stolen."

Then we heard it. The distant sound of sirens came closer and a police car and an ambulance whizzed past us. They stopped in a nearby parking lot and the ambulance attendants quickly ran into an apartment building, pulling a stretcher behind them. The next thing we knew, there was Gordon, calmly walking out of the apartment building, talking to the police. We ran over to him and listened while he explained what had happened.

"The thief took the suitcases back to his apartment and started unzipping them to see what he had stolen. I knew that I had to get out of there as fast as I could, so I was ready. When he threw back the lid of my suitcase, I

61

jumped out, screaming like a banshee and waving my arms. I guess the old guy's heart couldn't take the surprise. He had a heart-attack on the spot! I dialed 911 as the thief lay on the floor clutching his chest. The good news is, as the guy was lying there moaning, I took a minute to look around his apartment. He had all kinds of stuff in there – suitcases, briefcases, and best of all….THIS!" Gordon pulled a leather school bag out from behind his back and held it up for us to see. Inside were the english tests that our class had written!

Not only was Gordon a hero in the eyes of the police, but our class was thrilled not to have to write the test again. Mrs. Hoagsbrith celebrated the return of her leather school bag (and the safe return of Gordon) by buying the entire class a pizza lunch and promising us no more english tests for a whole month!

Chapter 10

The Mugger

It was almost the end of the school year and our class was going on a field trip to a museum in a city two hours away. There was a special section in the museum with really cool-looking dinosaur stuff that I was looking forward to, but I figured that the rest of the trip would be dull and boring. It turned out I was wrong.

As we boarded the bus, Mrs. Hoagsbrith collected our lunch money. We had all been told to bring $10.00 for lunch and admission to the museum, but our teacher said that she would hold the money for us until we got there. Coming from a small town, Mrs. Hoagsbrith didn't trust big cities, and I think she was afraid we would be mugged or something before we got to the restaurant. I handed over my money and watched Mrs. H. add it to her growing collection of ten dollar bills. When all the kids had paid, she folded the money and tucked it deep into the pocket of her jacket.

Two hours later we arrived at the museum. The bus parked in a large parking lot half a block away. We filed off the bus and waited in line until Mrs. Hoagsbrith got things organized. We were led across the crowded street toward the museum, and then it happened. Not looking as she rounded the corner, Mrs. Hoagsbrith walked right into the path of a jogger running at full speed. We watched in shocked silence as our teacher was knocked to the ground. The jogger landed right of top of her in a tangled heap of hands and feet! In a flash, the jogger jumped up and yelled, "Watch where you're going, old lady!" Then he took off down the street.

Mrs. Hoagsbrith lay on the ground, fumbling around for her glasses, which had been knocked off in the collision. Suddenly a worried look came over her face and she quickly reached into her jacket pocket.

"It's gone!" she shrieked. *"That jogger stole our*

money!"

"GET HIM!" shouted Gordon, and all 25 of us took off after the jogger, who was now a full block away.

People jumped out of the way as our class thundered down the sidewalk in hot pursuit of the mugger. The mugger heard the commotion and turned around to see an angry mob of kids racing after him. Coupled with war whoops and cries of *"**Mugger**,"* we must have been a scary sight. The jogger turned on the speed, but he was no match for 25 angry 12-year-olds. After all, he had knocked down our teacher on purpose, insulted her, and stolen our money! We were out for revenge. As our class drew closer to the mugger, Gordon launched a flying tackle at the thief and brought him to the ground! Half of our class fell on top of them, pinning the mugger to the ground by his legs and arms. The rest of us circled around him, growling and sneering.

"So," said Gordon. "You think you're pretty tough, knocking down old ladies! Funny, you don't seem so tough now." The mugger was too terrified to reply, and I could see his body trembling with fear.

"We want the money, and we want it now!" continued Gordon. "Hand it over and no one gets hurt!" The thief's arms were released and he quickly reached into his pocket and pulled out a wad of bills. Grabbing it, Gordon said, "OK, guys. You can let him go!" The mugger got up and ran off without so much as a backward glance.

Triumphantly we headed back down the street to where our teacher was just getting up with the help of some kind strangers. One of them had found her glasses and handed them to Mrs. Hoagsbrith.

"That's better," she sighed, straightening her rumpled clothing. As she did, she felt something bulging in the pocket of her skirt. "Oh, thank goodness," she breathed. "I didn't lose the money after all. Now I remember. I moved the money into my skirt pocket – the one with the zipper - for safe keeping. Well, no harm done, I guess."

We all glanced over at Gordon, who was just about to hand over the money to the teacher.

"None at all," he said, quickly tucking the wad of bills from the jogger into his own pocket. Several kids eyed each other guiltily. *Our class had just mugged an innocent jogger and stolen his money!* No one said a word as we quietly filed into the museum.

Chapter 11

The Day Gordon's Dad Ate Our Homework

It was a warm Friday afternoon in June. Our class was studying ecosystems, and Mrs. Hoagsbrith was taking us on a short field trip. Near our school there was a swamp where we had all played when we were little. Gordon, Paulo and I used to catch frogs and turtles there, but today we weren't going to the swamp to have fun. We were going there to study and learn about all the creatures that live there.

Because the swamp wasn't far from school, we walked there, and our route took us right past Gordon's house. Mr. Smith was outside cutting the grass. Our class waved and said hello. Mr. Smith, sweating in the hot afternoon sun, waved back. Down the street we trudged in our rubber boots, carrying nets and buckets. We were almost at the turnoff for the swamp, when someone at the back of the line called out, "Hey, there's a dog following us!" Everyone turned around.

"Oh, no!" groaned Gordon. "Chopper, what are you doing? Go back home!"

The dog, hearing his owner's voice, wagged his tail and trotted over to Gordon.

"Can he come with us?" several kids asked.

Mrs. Hoagsbrith sighed. "Well, since he's here now, he might as well. But Gordon," she warned. "You've got to keep an eye on him. The swamp is a delicate ecosystem, and I don't want that dog disturbing anything."

"He won't," promised Gordon. "I'll run back and get his leash!"

As our class walked down the dusty path to the swamp, Mrs. Hoagsbrith talked about all of the creatures that we might encounter.

"There are some geese nesting around here. I don't want anyone getting too close to their nests. Oh, I think I hear a bullfrog!"

Gordon rejoined the group, leading Chopper on his leash. The walk was actually very interesting. Mrs. H. knew a lot about frogs and turtles and tadpoles, and for the first time, everyone was paying close attention to what she was saying. We all stopped and looked as Mrs. Hoagsbrith pointed out various flowers and plants.

"This is skunk cabbage," Mrs. Hoagsbrith was saying. "And just around the bend, if we're lucky, we might get to see...." And then it happened. Her words faded away and she stopped suddenly, staring straight ahead in disbelief. We all followed her gaze. A few metres up the path was Chopper, his head buried in what looked like a nest built on the ground. Nearby, a goose was flapping its wings madly and honking loudly. Everyone turned and looked at Gordon, who was still holding the leash in one hand. On the end of the leash was an empty collar! Gordon rushed to the head of the group.

"NO! CHOPPER! *OUT OF THERE!*" he ordered. The dog looked up innocently. Dangling from its muzzle were some tiny, soft downy feathers. Our eyes travelled from Chopper's mouth down to the empty nest. *Uh-oh,* I thought. *Gordon's in trouble now. His dog just ate a nest full of baby geese!* Mrs. Hoagsbrith looked like she was about to faint. Her face turned white and she ordered Gordon to take his dog home immediately and stay there for the rest of the afternoon. Gordon meekly obeyed, and the rest of the class continued on to the pond.

"Now," said Mrs. Hoagsbrith in a voice that suddenly sounded tired and a little shaky, "I want everyone who brought a bucket to dip it into the water and scoop some out. We need to gather some samples in order for you to study the micro-organisms that we can't see with the naked eye."

After that, we hunted for frogs and turtles until Mrs. Hoagsbrith announced that it was time to gather up our things and head back to school.

Back in the classroom, we were each given a kit containing a magnifying glass, a plastic cup with a lid and a set of written instructions containing pictures of over 100 creatures that live in water. Our plastic cups were filled from the buckets of water we had collected at the pond. It was our homework to use the magnifying glass and see how many creatures we could identify in the water.

"Take the lids off when you get home and put your cups in a cool, dark place until you're ready to do your homework. That will make the organisms slow down slightly and they'll be easier to count," Mrs. Hoagsbrith instructed as we filed out the door.

I had an extra cup of water and a kit for Gordon. Paulo and I biked over to his house to deliver it. Mr. Smith was still outside fussing over his lawn when we arrived.

"Hey!" Gordon greeted us. "Did you see the look on the teacher's face when Chopper ate those goslings? I thought she was gonna die! Is she still mad?"

"I think she's over it. Here," I said. "I brought you your homework." I handed Gordon his kit containing the cup of water. "We're supposed to take the lids off and store the cups in a cool, dark place until we're ready to do our homework."

"Like that's gonna be anytime soon!" laughed Gordon.

"I know. Let's put all of our cups in the fridge to keep cool for now, and then let's do something fun."

With our cups safely tucked away in the fridge, we went outside to jump on Gordon's trampoline. It was so hot that within a few minutes we had worked up a sweat and headed back into the kitchen to find something cold to drink. And then it happened. As we entered the kitchen, there was Gordon's dad. He was standing in front of the fridge with the door still open. His head was tilted back as he drained a cold glass of water and placed it on the counter beside two other empty glasses – *the plastic glasses from our kits! Gordon's dad just drank our swamp water!!*

"Ahhh. That hit the spot," he said, wiping his mouth. "I sure worked up a thirst cutting the lawn today."

"Dad! You just drank our homework! That was swamp water!!" shouted Gordon.

Mr. Smith immediately turned a lovely shade of green and spent the rest of the day lying on the couch and running to the bathroom. For once, Gordon, Paulo and I had an honest excuse for not doing our homework.

Chapter 12

The Streakers

The Guinness Book of World Records states that the African Cheetah is the world's fastest land animal. Obviously, Guinness has never seen a streaking fourteen-year-old being chased by the police, a group of nuns and two stray dogs. Well, I have, and I'd put my money on the fourteen-year-old.

It all started one day while Gordon, Paulo and I were swimming in the river that runs through our town. We had been swimming there for years and we'd never had a problem. Unfortunately, that was about to change. As we splashed around in the water, cooling off on a particularly hot day, three tough-looking high-school kids showed up. They stood on the shore in their bathing suits, puffing on cigarettes and sizing us up. The largest of the three kids spoke first.

"I'm not swimming with a bunch of babies. Get out of the river now!" It was a command, not a suggestion.

Gordon, Paulo and I swam meekly ashore, climbed out of the water, put on our shoes and slunk away like beaten dogs. The three tough kids laughed at our retreating forms, chuckling as they slid into the cool water.

"We own this river now!" one of them shouted.
"Don't bother coming back!"

The prospect of a long hot summer with no swimming was depressing, but there didn't seem to be anything we could do about it. It was three of us against three of them, and they were bigger, older and tougher.

That evening, I got a call from Gordon.

"Don't ask why," he said. "I'll tell you tomorrow. Just meet me at my house first thing in the morning. We're going swimming. And make sure you wear two bathing suits, one on top of the other."

"Why *two* bathing suits?" I asked.

"I told you not to ask," said Gordon. "But it's my best idea ever. We're gonna reclaim our swimming spot!"

The next day, wearing two bathing suits each, Gordon, Paulo and I rode our bikes to the river. It was deserted; there was no sign of the tough kids. We swam and dove in the cool water. It felt great, but I couldn't help wondering what Gordon was planning. I also couldn't help stealing glances at the shore, waiting for the tough kids to show up. Sure enough, they did.

"HEY! What do you think you're doing here?" came an angry shout. **"We told you to stay away from our river!"**

They kicked off their shoes, flexed their muscles and waded into the water. They half-walked, half-swam toward us.

"I guess we'll have to teach you babies a lesson," the toughest-looking one said. His two friends grinned. I knew it was going to be a painful lesson that I didn't want to learn. *Thanks a lot, Gordon*, I thought miserably.

Suddenly Gordon called out, "Sure. You guys are bigger and stronger than us, and you can probably beat us up, but how **brave** are you?"

That stopped the three tough kids in their tracks.

"Braver than you, you little worm!" called out one of them, cracking his hairy knuckles.

"Brave enough to streak through town?" taunted Gordon. "How about a little dare? Whoever is brave enough to run through town naked gets the river." Gordon reached down into the water and pulled off his bathing suit - *one* of his bathing suits, that is. He waved it around in the air before throwing it ashore. Paulo and I did the same, making sure we only took off one of our bathing suits, leaving our second one on, hidden by the dark water. We threw them to shore. The three tough kids stood waist-deep in the river, looking at each other.

"What's the matter?" cried Gordon. "Are you chicken?" He started making chicken sounds and Paulo and I joined in.

Not to be outdone by us, the three tough kids reluctantly reached down and pulled off their own bathing suits and tossed them on shore.

"**NOW!**" shouted Gordon, and the three of us made a mad dash. We quickly grabbed all 6 bathing suits lying on shore, and wearing our second bathing suits, we leapt on our bikes and rode away as fast as we could. Turning around, I saw the three tough kids racing after us. They were waving their fists and shouting at us. We slowed down to let them catch up a bit, just to make them think they might actually catch us, and then we took off at top speed again.

Gordon headed downtown, with Paulo and me close behind. The streets were busy with the morning rush hour. Ahead of us on the sidewalk was a group of nuns, heading in our direction. We skilfully left the sidewalk and rode around them, with the tough kids right on our tail. There was shrieking and yelling as they ran right into the middle of the group of nuns. One of the nuns was knocked down, but the tough kids didn't even bother to stop to see if she was OK. Angry now, several of the nuns chased after the kids, trying to catch them. A couple of stray dogs got into the action, chasing the boys and

78

barking loudly. And then it happened. Two policemen were just leaving a donut shop when the naked boys whizzed passed them, followed by the angry nuns and stray dogs. They jumped into their car and turned on the siren and flashing lights, adding to the confusion. The tough kids were no longer interested in catching us. They were trying desperately to outrun the police. Within seconds, the car had caught up to the boys. The officers cornered the boys and demanded to know what was going on. From a safe distance, Gordon, Paulo and I could hear the red-faced kids being questioned by the police. Then they were loaded into the back of the cruiser and driven away.

I don't know what ever happened to the tough older kids. We figured they probably had to do some kind of community service to make up for knocking down a nun and for running through town naked, but they never bothered Gordon, Paulo and me again.

Chapter 13

Gordon's Bad Day

One day in July, Paulo and I rode our bikes over to Gordon's house. Gordon hadn't been feeling well for the past couple of days, and now that he was better, we were going to visit him. It was nothing too serious. His mother told us that he had the flu and diarrhea. Why do people always have to tell you when someone has diarrhea? I mean, is that really something you want people to know about? It had been a boring few days without Gordon and his crazy schemes to keep us busy, and we were glad that he was feeling like his old self again. Or was he?

When Paulo and I pulled into the driveway, we could see Gordon sitting quietly on his front porch swing.

Gordon never just sat quietly, so I figured he must still be under the weather.

As if reading my mind, Paulo whispered, "He must still be sick. Don't get too close in case you catch it."

We climbed the porch steps and sat down on two chairs across from Gordon.

"How're you doing?" I asked.

"Oh, I feel fine. Perfect, in fact," said Gordon

"Then why are you just sitting here?" asked Paulo. "Let's go do something fun."

"You guys go on without me," answered Gordon glumly.

"What's the matter?" I asked. "You still sick?"

With a sigh and a slight shudder, Gordon said, "Yesterday was the worst day of my life!"

"What happened?" demanded Paulo. I had to admit that I was curious, too.

"There I was, sick in bed with the flu. I had a high fever and my stomach was killing me. My mom said that she couldn't stay home with me because she had to go to work. My dad was at work, too. Even my sisters were at

Day Camp."

"Well, you *are* twelve. Being home alone sick isn't all that bad when you're twelve," I said.

"No. That's not the bad part," said Gordon.

"Well, then what is?" asked Paulo.

"Before she left for work, my mother asked me to take a casserole out of the freezer to defrost. My grandmother was coming over for dinner."

"I thought you liked your grandmother?" I said.

"I do. That's not the worst part. I fell asleep and woke up six hours later, all hot and sweaty, so I decided to take a shower. When I got out of the shower, there were no towels in the bathroom closet."

"I hate when that happens," I agreed. "But what's so bad about that?"

"That's still not the worst part," said Gordon. "I had to walk wet and naked through the entire house to go down to the basement and get a towel out of the dryer."

"Well, at least no one was at home to see you," said Paulo.

"It gets worse," insisted Gordon. "When I got

downstairs, I saw the freezer and remembered that I was supposed to have taken out that casserole hours ago. It would never defrost in time for dinner."

"So what?" I interrupted. "Then you get to eat out! That's what we do when my mom doesn't feel like cooking."

"Listen," said Gordon. "It gets worse. I opened the lid to the chest freezer, and naturally, there was no casserole. None that I could see, anyway. So I started rooting around trying to find it. I figured it was buried on the bottom of the freezer. I reached deep into the freezer and started digging around, and then it happened."

"What happened? What'd you do, fall in?" I asked. The story was finally getting good.

"NO!" shouted Gordon. "I didn't fall in! I got stuck. I was wet and hot from the shower, and probably the fever, too. I was on my tiptoes, reaching to the bottom of the freezer and my hands touched the inside of the freezer! They froze instantly. I was stuck! You know, like that time in the winter when you got your tongue stuck to the pole when you were about six?"

83

I grimaced, remembering how much it had hurt to pull my tongue off the cold steel pole. "Ouch," I said with sympathy. "That must have been awful!"

"Oh, but it gets worse! There I was, stuck to the inside of the freezer, unable to pull my hands off, and all of a sudden I heard voices. My mother was home!"

Paulo and I laughed hysterically.

"You mean that your mother had to come and rescue you? And you were buck naked?" cried Paulo. "That *is* the worst thing that could happen!"

"Oh, but there's more," continued Gordon. "My mother had picked up my sisters and some of their friends from Day Camp on her way home from work!" Paulo and I laughed even harder.

"*AND MY GRANDMOTHER WAS WITH THEM, TOO!*"

We fell off our chairs in a fit of hysterics.

"And because my sisters were all muddy from playing soccer, they used the basement entrance! *They opened the door and were greeted by my bare butt sticking out*

84

of the freezer!! How's that for embarrassing??" he practically shouted.

When we could speak again, Paulo said, "You're right, Gordon. That is absolutely, positively, without a doubt the worst thing that could ever happen to anyone!"

"And it couldn't have happened to a nicer guy," I added.

About the Authors

Michael Wade was born a long time ago, in a place far, far away. He grew up in London, Ontario and currently lives in Strathroy, Ontario. Michael enjoys hunting, wilderness canoeing and working out.

Laura Wade was born not quite so long ago and not as far away as Michael. She, too, was raised in London, Ontario and currently resides in Strathroy, where she works as a Children's Librarian.

Catch All The Exciting Adventures of Gordon, Paulo and Me!

Order the complete
And Then It Happened
series today.

For details on ordering books,
student activities, new stories and more,
visit us at our Web Site
www.boysbookshelf.com